Why I Love My Mummy

Illustrated by Daniel Howarth

HarperCollins *Children's Books*

I love my mummy because...

she holds my hand.

I love my mummy because...

she takes me to nice places.

I love my mummy because...

she plays with me.

I love my mummy because...

She helps me.

I love my mummy because...

she kisses me better.

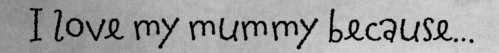

I love my mummy because...

she feeds me.

I love my mummy because...

she gives me a bath.

I love my mummy because...

she sings to me.

I love my mummy because...

she always hugs me.

I love my mummy because...

she helps me sleep at night.

Everyone loves their mummy –

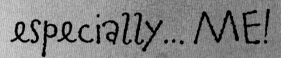

especially... ME!

First published in hardback in Great Britain by HarperCollins Children's Books in 2006
First published in paperback in 2013
This edition published in 2019

3 5 7 9 10 8 6 4 2

978-0-00-797700-0

HarperCollins Children's Books is a division of HarperCollins Publishers Ltd.

Text and illustrations copyright © HarperCollins Publishers Ltd 2006

A CIP catalogue record for this title is available from the British Library.

Visit our website at www.harpercollins.co.uk

Printed in China